This book belongs to

_____

Disney · PIXAR

A READ-ALOUD STORYBOOK

ADAPTED BY
LISA MARSOLI

ILLUSTRATED BY
CAROLINE EGAN, OLGA MOSQUEDA,
ELENA NAGGI, AND SCOTT TILLEY,
AND THE DISNEY STORYBOOK ARTISTS

DESIGNED BY
DEBORAH BOONE

Random House  New York

Copyright © 2009 Disney Enterprises, Inc./Pixar. All rights reserved. Published in the United States by Random House Children's Books, a division of Random House, Inc., 1745 Broadway, New York, NY 10019, and in Canada by Random House of Canada Limited, Toronto, in conjunction with Disney Enterprises, Inc. Random House and the colophon are registered trademarks of Random House, Inc.
Library of Congress Control Number: 2008934569   ISBN: 978-0-7364-2572-8
www.randomhouse.com/kids

Printed in the United States of America
10 9 8 7 6 5 4 3 2 1

The lights in the movie theater dimmed, and the film started to roll. Young Carl Fredricksen gazed up at the screen in awe. There, larger than life, was his idol— Charles Muntz, the world-famous explorer.

The newsreel showed Muntz boarding his custom-made airship, the *Spirit of Adventure*, accompanied by his trusty dogs. They were off to South America to capture a creature known as the Monster of Paradise Falls. "Adventure is out there!" Muntz declared.

Carl wanted to be an adventurer when he grew up, just like Charles Muntz!

That afternoon, Carl wrote *Spirit of Adventure* on a balloon and pretended it was his own airship. While he was playing, he heard someone exclaim, "Adventure is out there!" Carl stopped in his tracks. That was exactly what Charles Muntz always said! The voice seemed to be coming from inside an old, empty house.

Carl went into the house to investigate. A girl named Ellie was flying her own make-believe airship!

"Don't you know this is an exclusive club? Only explorers get in here!" Ellie cried. She startled Carl so badly he let go of his balloon.

Ellie quickly realized that Carl was an explorer, too. So she fastened a pin made from a grape-soda bottle cap to his shirt. "You and me, we're in a club now," she told him.

Carl and Ellie soon had their very first adventure together: Carl fell and broke his arm! That night, Ellie came by his house to cheer him up. She brought her adventure book to show him.

"I'm going where Charles Muntz is going: South America," Ellie explained. She pointed to a picture she'd made of her clubhouse sitting right next to Paradise Falls. The pages after that were blank. "I'm saving these for all the adventures I'm gonna have," she told Carl.

Ellie made Carl promise to take them to Paradise Falls someday. "Swear you'll take us. Cross your heart!" she ordered.

Carl did. He thought Ellie was quite a girl.

Carl and Ellie were best friends from that moment on. When they grew up, they got married and moved into the old place that had been their clubhouse. They fixed up their home to look just like the drawing in Ellie's adventure book.

But Carl and Ellie didn't become explorers. They both worked at the zoo. Carl sold balloons from a cart, and Ellie looked after the animals in the South America house.

However, they still dreamed of traveling to Paradise Falls. They saved all their spare change in a jar to pay for the trip. But they could never quite collect enough.

The years went by, and Carl and Ellie grew older. After Ellie passed away, Carl kept all her things just as they had been. But it wasn't the same. He missed Ellie.

To make matters worse, the neighborhood around their beloved home was being torn down to make room for modern high-rises.

One day, Carl heard a knock at his door. A boy in a uniform was standing on his porch. "Good afternoon," said the boy. "My name is Russell, and I am a Junior Wilderness Explorer. Are you in need of assistance today, sir?"

"No," replied Carl. He didn't want help. He just wanted to be left alone.

But Russell wouldn't leave. He wanted to help Carl so that he could earn his Assisting the Elderly badge. "If I get it, I will become a Senior Wilderness Explorer," Russell explained.

To get rid of Russell, Carl gave him an impossible task. He asked him to find a bird called a snipe. "I think its burrow is two blocks down," Carl said.

Russell eagerly set off to find the bird, not knowing it didn't exist. Carl had made the whole thing up!

Not long after that, Carl received some bad news. He was being forced out of his house and sent to live in a retirement home. Carl didn't want to leave his house. All his memories of Ellie were there.

That night, Carl sat in his living room, looking through Ellie's adventure book. He remembered Ellie's dream of going to South America.

The next morning, two nurses arrived to drive Carl to the retirement home.

"I'll meet you at the van. I want to say one last goodbye to the old place," Carl told them, handing over his suitcase.

As the nurses walked back to their van, a huge shadow fell over them. They turned to see thousands of balloons tied to Carl's house. A moment later, the whole house rose into the air.

"So long, boys!" Carl yelled out the window.

Carl steered the flying house using ropes attached to the weather vane. He checked his compass and map and charted a course to Paradise Falls in South America. "We're on our way, Ellie," he said happily.

Suddenly, there was a knock at the door. Carl was shocked. He was thousands of feet up in the air! Who could be at his door?

It was Russell! He'd been under Carl's porch, looking for the snipe, when the house lifted off. "Please let me in!" Russell begged.

What choice did Carl have? He let Russell come inside.

Carl hated to stop, but he knew he had to land and send Russell home. He started to cut some of the balloons free.

Meanwhile, Russell was watching the clouds out the window. "There's a big storm coming," he said. But Carl didn't hear him.

A flash of lightning lit up the room. Carl desperately tried to steer the house away from the storm, but it was too late. The little house tossed in the wind. Carl ran this way and that, trying to save Ellie's belongings.

Finally, exhausted, he fell asleep.

When Carl woke up, the storm was over. "I steered us down," Russell told him proudly. "We're in South America."

As Carl and Russell stepped out onto the porch, the house crash-landed and sent them both flying.

"My house!" Carl cried as it started to drift away. Grabbing hold of the garden hose, he and Russell managed to pull the house back down.

Just then, the fog cleared. There, a short distance ahead, was Paradise Falls. It looked just like Ellie's picture! "We made it!" Carl shouted. "We could float right over there!"

There was just one problem: they couldn't get back into the house. It was hovering too high off the ground.

Russell had an idea: they could *walk* the house to the falls. They made harnesses out of the garden hose so they could pull the house.

"This is fun already, isn't it?" Russell said as they trudged along. "Don't you worry," he told Carl, "I'm gonna assist you every step of the way."

After a while, they stopped to take a break. As Russell nibbled a chocolate bar, a beak poked out of the bushes and began to nibble it, too!

"Don't be afraid," Russell told the creature. He used more chocolate to lure it from its hiding spot.

When the creature emerged, Russell gasped. It was the biggest bird he had ever seen!

The bird liked chocolate. It liked Russell, too. Russell named the bird Kevin. He couldn't wait to show his new friend to Carl!

"Aiigh!" Carl yelled when he saw the bird. "What is that thing?"

"It's a snipe!" Russell answered. "Can we keep him?"

"No," said Carl.

Carl and Russell set off for Paradise Falls again. But Russell didn't want to leave Kevin behind, so he dropped a trail of chocolate for the bird to follow.

They hadn't gone far when they met a dog.

"Hi there," said the dog. "My name is Dug."

A talking dog? Carl and Russell were stunned!

"My master made me this collar so that I may talk," Dug explained. "My pack sent me on a special mission. Have you seen a bird? I want to find one. I have been on the scent."

Suddenly, Kevin flew out of the bushes and tackled Dug.

"Hey, that is the bird! May I take your bird back to camp as my prisoner?" Dug asked Carl.

"Yes! Yes! Take it!" Carl told him.

Russell wanted to keep Dug as a pet. "No," said Carl.

"But he's a talking dog!" Russell exclaimed.

Carl didn't want a talking dog. He didn't want a bird, either. He just wanted to get to the falls. Russell followed Carl, Kevin followed Russell, and Dug followed the bird.

"Please be my prisoner," Dug begged Kevin.

That night, they stopped to rest. "Dug says he wants to take Kevin prisoner. We have to protect him!" Russell told Carl while the others slept.

Carl agreed that Kevin could come with them to the falls.

"Promise you won't leave Kevin? Cross your heart?" Russell asked Carl.

Carl thought for a moment. The last time he'd crossed his heart was when he'd promised Ellie he would take her to Paradise Falls.

"Cross my heart," he finally told Russell.

The next morning, they found Kevin perched on the roof. The bird was calling toward the distant rocks.

"The bird is calling to her babies," Dug explained.

"Kevin's a *girl*?" Russell asked in surprise.

Soon Kevin set off for her home. Russell wanted to go with her. But Carl was in a hurry to get to the falls. "She can take care of herself," he told Russell.

Suddenly, three fierce dogs burst from the bushes. They surrounded Carl, Russell, and Dug, and demanded the bird. The dogs were part of Dug's pack.

When they discovered that Dug had lost the bird, they insisted on taking the travelers back to their master.

The dogs led Carl and Russell to an enormous cave. An old man stood in the entrance, surrounded by more vicious-looking dogs.

When the man saw Carl's house, he laughed. He had thought that Carl and Russell were explorers—but real explorers wouldn't come in a floating house! "My dogs made a mistake," he told Carl, and started to leave.

Carl thought the man looked familiar. "Wait," he said. "Are you . . . Charles Muntz?"

"Adventure is out there!" Muntz replied.

Carl couldn't believe he was finally meeting his childhood hero. "My wife and I, we're your biggest fans!" he said, shaking Muntz's hand.

Muntz was pleased to have visitors after so many years. He invited Carl and Russell inside to rest. A giant airship was parked in the cave. Carl recognized it right away—it was the *Spirit of Adventure*!

When Dug tried to follow Carl and Russell into the airship, the other dogs blocked his way.

"He has lost the bird," declared Alpha, the leader of the pack. "Put him in the Cone of Shame."

Dug was left outside wearing his humiliating punishment. "I do not like the Cone of Shame," he said sadly.

On board the airship, the dogs served dinner while Muntz
told Carl and Russell about the Monster of Paradise Falls.
"I've spent a lifetime tracking this creature," Muntz said,
showing them his research.

"Hey, that looks like Kevin!" said Russell, noticing a bird
skeleton.

"Kevin?" Muntz asked, startled.

"That's my new giant bird pet," Russell explained.
"I trained it to follow us."

Muntz became very angry. He thought Carl and Russell
were trying to steal the bird from him.

At that moment, they heard a wail outside. Kevin had followed Carl and Russell into the cave!

All the dogs began to bark. In the confusion, Carl and Russell slipped away.

"Get them!" Muntz roared at his dogs.

Carl and Russell untied the house and started to run. The snarling dog pack came tearing down the gangplank after them.

Kevin scooped Russell and Carl onto her back and raced for the cave opening, with the house still floating behind.

But Kevin wasn't fast enough to stay ahead of the pack. The dogs were closing in.

Suddenly, an avalanche of rocks tumbled down and blocked the dog pack. "Go on, Master. I will stop the dogs!" someone cried.

It was Dug! He had come to rescue Carl and Russell.

But Dug didn't stop the pack for long. Alpha shoved him aside and jumped between the rocks.

Up ahead, Carl, Russell, and Kevin had come to the edge of a cliff. They were trapped!

Luckily, the wind lifted the house into the air—taking Carl and his friends with it! Alpha clamped down on Kevin's leg to try to stop them, but he lost his grip. The house floated over the gap to safety, while the dogs plummeted into the water below.

Carl and his friends had escaped, but Kevin's leg was badly injured. Russell realized that the bird needed help to get back to her babies.

Out of nowhere, a spotlight appeared and shone down on the bird. Muntz had followed them in the *Spirit of Adventure*!

Before Kevin could escape, a net shot from the airship and trapped her. Carl sawed at the net with Russell's pocketknife, trying to set her free.

"Get away from my bird!" Muntz snarled. Then he set Carl's house on fire!

Carl couldn't let his house go up in smoke—it held all his memories of Ellie. So he gave up Kevin instead. The dogs dragged the wounded bird onto the airship.

As Muntz lifted off with his prize bird, Carl ran to his house and beat back the flames.

"You gave away Kevin," Russell accused Carl.

Carl felt terrible, but what could he do? "I didn't ask for any of this!" he snapped. "And if you hadn't shown up," he told Dug, "none of this would have happened. Bad dog!"

Dug slunk away with his tail between his legs.

"Now," Carl declared to Russell, "whether you assist me or not, I am going to Paradise Falls if it kills me."

Russell did not help Carl this time. So Carl towed the house the rest of the way to Paradise Falls by himself. He placed the house exactly where it appeared in Ellie's drawing.

Russell was still angry with Carl. "Here," he said bitterly, throwing his Wilderness Explorer sash on the ground. "I don't want this anymore."

With a sigh, Carl picked up Russell's sash and went into his house.

Carl found Ellie's adventure book and put her drawing back inside. He had kept his promise. But he still felt sad. He wished Ellie were there with him.

Carl started to close the book, but something caught his eye. It was a photograph of their wedding day. Carl turned the page. He had never looked through the whole book before. To his astonishment, it was filled with photographs of the two of them over the years.

On the last page, there was a message from Ellie: *Thanks for the adventure. Now go have one of your own.*

Carl smiled, realizing that Ellie had gotten her wish after all. Their life together had been the adventure.

Suddenly, Carl heard something on the roof. He hurried outside and saw Russell gripping a bunch of balloons.

"I'm gonna help Kevin, even if you won't!" Russell cried as he rose into the air. He zoomed away, using a leaf blower to steer.

"No, Russell!" Carl shouted. He knew he had to go after Russell before something terrible happened. But the house wouldn't budge. The balloons had lost too much air.

Carl threw a chair off the porch in frustration. The house bobbed a little. That gave him an idea. He began throwing his belongings out of the house to make it lighter. Carl had realized he didn't need those things— Russell was more important!

Slowly, the house began to rise. Carl was on his way!

As Carl was scanning the sky for any sign of Russell, he heard a knock at the door.

"Russell?" he asked hopefully.

But this time, it was Dug. "I was hiding on your porch because I love you. Can I stay?" he asked.

"Well, you're my dog, aren't you?" replied Carl. "And I'm your master!"

Dug was overjoyed. Together he and Carl set out to rescue Russell.

Carl flew through a cloud and saw the *Spirit of Adventure* just ahead. As he watched, the gangplank slowly lowered in midair. Something was sliding down it.

Suddenly, Carl realized it was Russell! The boy was tied to a chair—and he was about to fall into thin air!

Carl grabbed the garden hose. Using it like a rope, he swung over to the airship and caught Russell just before he fell.

Once Russell was safe inside the house, Carl and Dug went back for Kevin. Muntz had locked the bird in a cage guarded by his dog pack.

Carl grabbed a tennis ball from his cane. "Who wants the ball?" he called to dogs.

"I do! I do!" The dogs jumped up and down.

Carl threw the ball, and the dogs chased it—right out the door. Carl locked the door behind them, then set Kevin free.

Suddenly, Muntz appeared, swinging a sword. Carl blocked it with his cane. The two old men fought, cane and sword clashing.

Meanwhile, outside, Russell was having his own problems. He'd accidentally fallen from the house. As he dangled from the end of the garden hose, dogs in fighter planes buzzed around him, trying to bring the house down.

Finally, Carl escaped from Muntz. He made it back to the house with Dug and Kevin. They had just started to fly away when—*bang!* Balloons popped, and the house plunged downward. It struck the top of the airship, and Carl fell out.

Muntz saw his chance. He charged into the house to get the bird.

The house began to slide toward the edge of the airship. Carl had to save his friends! "Hang on to Kevin!" he yelled to Russell and Dug. Pulling a bar of chocolate from his pocket, Carl waved it and cried, "Bird, chocolate!"

Kevin ran toward the chocolate, dragging Russell and Dug behind her. They made it to the airship just before the house fell.

Muntz, however, wasn't so lucky. His foot caught on a bunch of balloons, and he drifted up and away.

"Sorry about your house, Mr. Fredricksen," Russell said as they watched it disappear into the clouds.

"You know," said Carl, "it's just a house." It didn't seem as important to him, now that he had friends.

Carl and his friends helped Kevin get back to her family. After a visit with the fuzzy little chicks, it was time to go.

They called goodbye to Kevin, then climbed aboard the *Spirit of Adventure*. Carl and Russell were going home, too.

Back home, Russell received his final badge and became a Senior Wilderness Explorer. Carl came to the ceremony to pin the badge on him.

"Russell, for assisting the elderly, and for performing above and beyond the call of duty, I would like to award you the highest honor I can bestow: the Ellie badge," Carl said. He fastened the grape-soda-cap pin to Russell's sash.

"Wow!" Russell cried. Carl smiled, knowing that he and his new friends had many exciting adventures ahead of them.